Oxford Progressive English Readers
General Editor: D.H. Howe

A Christmas Carol

The *Oxford Progressive English Readers* series provides a wide range of reading for learners of English. It includes classics, the favourite stories of young readers, and also modern fiction. The series has five grades: the *Introductory Grade* at a 1400 word level, *Grade 1* at a 2100 word level, *Grade 2* at a 3100 word level, *Grade 3* at a 3700 word level and *Grade 4* which consists of abridged stories. Structural as well as lexical controls are applied at each level.

Wherever possible the mood and style of the original stories have been retained. Where this requires departure from the grading scheme, definitions and notes are given.

All the books in the series are attractively illustrated. Each book also has a short section containing questions and suggested activities for students.

A Christmas Carol

Charles Dickens

Hong Kong
OXFORD UNIVERSITY PRESS
Oxford Singapore Tokyo

Oxford University Press

Oxford New York Toronto
Petaling Jaya Singapore Hong Kong Tokyo
Delhi Bombay Calcutta Madras Karachi
Nairobi Dar es Salaam Cape Town
Melbourne Auckland

and associated companies in
Beirut Berlin Ibadan Nicosia

© Oxford University Press 1975
First published 1975
Ninth impression 1987

OXFORD is a trade mark of Oxford University Press

Retold by A. Sweaney
Illustrated by Rosemary Parsons
Cover illustration by Kathryn Blomfield
Simplified according to the language grading scheme
especially compiled by D.H. Howe

ISBN 0 19 580724 3

Printed in Hong Kong by Kwong Fat Offset Printing Co. Ltd.
Published by Oxford University Press, Warwick House, Hong Kong

Contents

1 Scrooge of 'Scrooge and Marley'

When our story begins, Marley was dead. He had been dead for a long time. Of course Scrooge knew he was dead. Scrooge and he had worked together for many years, and Scrooge was his only friend. Marley's death was sad, but Scrooge did not cry for long. On the day 5 Marley was buried, Scrooge was still a good businessman.

Scrooge never painted out Marley's name. There it stood for years afterwards over the office door — SCROOGE AND MARLEY. The business was known as *Scrooge and Marley*. People who did not know the busi- 10 ness sometimes called Scrooge 'Scrooge', and sometimes 'Marley', but he answered to both names. It was all the same to him.

Scrooge never gave away anything. He was as secret as a fish. He had a cold heart and an unfriendly face, a 15 pointed nose, red eyes and thin blue lips. There was snow on his head and over his eyes and on his mouth. He carried bad weather about with him.

Nobody ever came to him in the street, saying with a happy face, 'My dear Scrooge, how are you? When 20 will you come to see me?' No beggar asked him for money. No children asked him what time it was. No man or woman ever asked Scrooge the way to any place. Even the blind men's dogs seemed afraid of him. When they saw him coming they would pull their owners out 25 of the way until he had passed. But do you think Scrooge cared? It was the thing he liked most!

Scrooge's nephew visits him

Then, one Christmas Eve, the best day of the year,

old Scrooge sat busy in his office. It was cold, dark,
December weather. Outside, the people in the street
were walking up and down. They stamped their feet on
the road to keep themselves warm. The city clocks had
5 just struck three, but it was quite dark already. It had
not been light all day.

The door of his office was open, because he was
watching his clerk in the next room. Scrooge had a very
small fire. The clerk's fire was even smaller and looked
10 like one piece of coal. The clerk had put on his long
scarf* to keep himself warm.

'A Happy Christmas, Uncle, God save you!' cried a
bright voice. It was the voice of Scrooge's nephew. This
was the first knowledge Scrooge had of his coming,
15 because he came in so quickly.

'Bah!' said Scrooge. 'Go away! Go away!'

Scrooge's nephew was quite warm from walking quickly in the December cold. His face was red and good
to look at. His eyes shone and his breath smoked in the
20 cold air.

'You're telling me to go away at Christmas, Uncle,'
said Scrooge's nephew. 'You don't mean that, I'm sure.'

'I do ,' said Scrooge. 'Bah! Happy Christmas! Why are
you happy? You're poor enough.'

25 'Why are you *unhappy*?' said the nephew, laughing.
'You're *rich* enough.'

Scrooge said 'Bah' again, and followed it by saying
'Go away.' He had no better answers at the moment.

'Don't be angry, Uncle,' the nephew said.

30 'What else can I be,' replied his uncle, 'when I live in
this world of foolish people? Happy Christmas! Bah to a
Happy Christmas! What is Christmas time to you but a
time for paying bills without money? A time when you
find yourself a year older and not an hour richer.'

35 Scrooge went on, 'A man who goes about saying "A

scarf, long piece of woollen cloth worn around the neck.

Happy Christmas" is a fool. Why not boil him with his own pudding, and bury him with a branch of holly* through his heart?'

'Uncle!' cried the nephew.

'Nephew!' returned the uncle. 'Enjoy Christmas in 5
your own way, and let me enjoy it in my way.'

'Enjoy it, Uncle!' repeated Scrooge's nephew. 'But you don't enjoy it.'

'Let me leave it alone, then,' said Scrooge. 'It has never done you much good!' 10

The nephew said, 'I know there are many things from which I have not earned money. Christmas is one of these things. But I have always thought of Christmas as a time to love, forgive and be kind. Christmas is a good and pleasant time. It is the only time in the long seasons 15
of the year when men and women talk to each other freely. A time when people think of others as their friends through life, and not strangers making different journeys. And therefore, Uncle, though Christmas has never put a piece of gold or silver into my pocket, I 20
believe that it has done me good. And I say, "May God make Christmas happy." '

The clerk in the small office in the next room spoke loudly in agreement. When he thought about what he had done, he turned the coal in the fire over. The last 25
bit of warmth was destroyed for ever.

'Let me have another sign from you,' said Scrooge to the clerk, 'and you'll keep your Christmas by losing your work.' Then he turned to his nephew. 'You are quite clever with your speech, sir. I am surprised you 30
don't go into Parliament*.'

'Don't be angry, Uncle. Come, have your lunch with us tomorrow.'

*holly, plant with green shiny leaves.
*Parliament, the British government.

Scrooge said that he would never do that.

'But why?' cried Scrooge's nephew. 'Why?'

'Why did you get married?' said Scrooge.

'Because I fell in love.'

5 'Because you fell in love!' repeated Scrooge, thinking love the one thing more foolish than 'A Happy Christmas'. 'Good afternoon!'

'I am really sorry that you will not change your ideas. There has been nothing to separate us. I came to you

10 because it was Christmas. I'll keep my Christmas kindness to the last. So, a Happy Christmas, Uncle.'

'Good afternoon!'

'And a Happy New Year!'

'Good afternoon!'

15 His nephew left the room without an angry word. He went to the clerk to wish him a Happy Christmas. Though the clerk was cold, he was warmer than Scrooge because he returned the greeting happily.

20 'There's another fool,' thought Scrooge, who heard their words. 'My clerk with fifteen shillings* a week and a wife and family, talking about a Happy Christmas. I believe the world

25 is going mad.'

A visit from two gentlemen collecting money for the poor

When the clerk let Scrooge's nephew out, he had let two other people

shilling, an English coin.

in. They were big gentlemen who were pleasant to look at. They now stood, with their hats off, in Scrooge's office. They had books and papers in their hands, and they bowed to him.

5   'Scrooge and Marley, I believe,' said one of the gentlemen, looking at his papers. 'Am I talking to Mr Scrooge or Mr Marley?'

'Mr Marley has been dead for seven years,' Scrooge replied. 'He died seven years ago on this very night.'

10   'We are sure that his partner has the same kindness,' said the gentlemen, handing some papers to Scrooge. (He certainly did have the same kindness. Marley had been as unwilling to give away money as Scrooge.)

'At this time of the year,' said the gentleman, taking

15   a pen, 'it is very necessary that we try to help the poor, and all who are in need of help. There are great numbers of these people — every one of them in need of food and warmth.'

'Are there no prisons?' asked Scrooge.

20   'Plenty of prisons,' said the gentleman, putting down his pen.

'And workhouses* — are there plenty of those?'

'There are, but I wish I could say there were not!'

'I was afraid, from your first words, that something

25   had closed them!'

'Well, the workhouses do not give comfort to the great numbers of people outside them. We are trying to get some money to buy meat and drink and warmth for them. We chose this time of the year because it is the

30   time when poor people feel most unhappy. What will you give, Mr Scrooge?'

*workhouses, homes where poor people could live and work. Conditions in these homes in Dickens' time were very bad.

'Nothing,' Scrooge replied.

'Do you mean that? You do not wish to give any money?'

'I wish to be left alone,' said Scrooge. 'You ask me what I wish, gentlemen, and that is my answer. I am not   5
happy myself at Christmas, and I have no money to make other people happy. I help the prisons and the workhouses with my money, and they cost enough. Those poor you speak of can go there!'

'Many can't go there, and many would rather die than   10
go there.'

'If they would rather die, then let them do it. The numbers of the poor will grow less. But I don't believe that they would rather die.'

'But you might believe it.'   15

'It's not my business,' Scrooge replied. 'It's enough for a man to understand his own business, and not to trouble about other people's. Good afternoon, gentlemen!'

The gentlemen saw that it would be useless to say   20
anything more, and went away. Scrooge went on with his work. He felt very pleased and much happier than he usually was.

Scrooge closes his office for Christmas

It was darker and colder. Both outside and in, there was a sharp, biting cold. A child's voice sang a Christmas   25
song through the key-hole* of Scrooge's office.

Scrooge reached for a ruler so quickly that the small singer ran away in fear. Once more the key-hole was left to the cold and wind.

At last it was time to close the office. Scrooge angrily   30
climbed out of his chair. He told the waiting clerk that he could leave his work. He put on his hat.

*key-hole, the part of the door in which one puts the key.

'You want to be at home all tomorrow, I believe?' said Scrooge.

'If it is all right, sir.'

'It's not all right, and it's not fair. If I take some
5 money from you for doing it, you will think badly of me, I'm quite sure.'

The clerk smiled.

'And yet,' said Scrooge, 'you don't think that I am badly treated when I pay you a day's money for doing
10 no work.'

The clerk said that it was only once a year.

'That's a poor excuse for taking a man's money every twenty-fifth of December,' said Scrooge. He pulled his overcoat well round his neck. 'All right, then, you must
15 have the whole day. Come here much earlier the next morning.'

The clerk promised that he would, and walked out. In a second, the office was closed. The ends of the clerk's scarf hung below his waist, for *he* had no overcoat. He
20 slid down the ice in the road, at the end of a line of boys, twenty times because it was Christmas. Then he ran home to Camden Town as fast as he could, to play Christmas games with his children.

Scrooge sees Marley's face

Scrooge ate his dinner alone in his usual restaurant.
25 He read all the newspapers, and amused himself by reading his bank book. He left the restaurant and went home to go to bed.

He lived in the same rooms that he had once shared with his friend Marley. They were a dark, dull set of
30 rooms, in a dark building, up many dark stairs. Only Scrooge lived there, for the other rooms were all used as offices during the day.

He knew every stone on the path of that black place. It was so dark that he had to feel his way with his hand until he reached his door.

There was nothing at all unusual about the knocker* on the door, except that it was very large. Scrooge had *5* seen it every night and every morning during the time that he had lived in the place. Scrooge never imagined things. Can any man explain what happened next? Scrooge put the key in the door. Then he saw in the knocker, not a knocker, but Marley's face! *10*

Marley's face! It was not as dark as the other things in the yard were. There was a pale light about it, like a bad fish in a dark room! It was not angry or wicked. It looked at Scrooge just as Marley used to look, with his glasses pushed up over his head. His hair was moving *15* strangely, as if by breath or hot air. The eyes were wide open, but they did not move. That, and the strange light, made it frightening to look at. As Scrooge's eyes were upon it, it changed into a knocker again.

Scrooge was very surprised. In fact, his blood was *20* cold with fright. But he put his hand on the key, and turned it firmly. Then he walked in and lit his lamp.

He did not stop for a moment before he shut the door. He did look carefully behind it first. But there was nothing on the door at all. He said 'Bah!' and closed the *25* door with a loud noise.

The noise sounded through the house like thunder. Every room above, and every box in the rooms below, made its own special noise. But Scrooge was not afraid of noises. He fastened the door and walked across the *30* hall. He went up the stairs slowly, holding up his lamp. He closed his door and locked himself in, which was not usual. In this way he felt safe. He took off his collar and

*knocker, a heavy bar on the outside of a door, used instead of a doorbell many years ago.

tie and coat, and put on a long loose coat, and slippers*, and his night-cap. Then he sat down before his fire to take his usual evening drink.

The ghost* of Marley appears before Scrooge

Scrooge rested his head on the back of his chair. By chance, his eyes saw a bell that hung in the room. The   5
bell was never used and nobody remembered why it was there. Scrooge was suddenly afraid. As he looked at it, he saw this bell begin to move. It moved so softly at first that it did not make a sound. Soon, however, it rang out very loudly, and so did every bell in the house.   10

This lasted perhaps half a minute, or a minute, but it seemed an hour. The bells finished, as they had begun, all together. They were followed by a noise deep down below. Was someone dragging a heavy chain? Then Scrooge thought about ghosts. People say that, in some   15
houses, ghosts pull chains along.

'Bah! Go away!' said Scrooge. He heard a door below burst open with a great sound. Then he heard the noise much louder coming up the stairs, straight towards his door.   20

'It's nonsense still,' said Scrooge, 'I won't believe it.' His colour soon changed. Without stopping, the ghost came on through the heavy doors. It passed into the room before his eyes. When it came in, the dying flame in the fire jumped up. The flame cried, 'I know him!   25
Marley's ghost,' and fell again.

The same face, the very same face. Marley in his usual clothes and boots. The chain was fastened around his middle. It was long and went about him like a tail. Scrooge examined it very carefully. It was made of   30
money-boxes, keys, bank-books, and heavy boxes. He

*slippers, soft house-shoes.
*ghost, a dead person appearing to the living.

could see right through the
body of the ghost. As he was
looking at its belt, he could
see the two buttons on the
coat behind it.   *5*

Scrooge talks to Marley's ghost
    'What now?' said Scrooge,
as hard and cold as ever. 'What
do you want with me?'
    'Much,' said Marley's voice.
    'Who are you?'   *10*
    'Ask me who I *was.*'
    'Who were you then?' said
Scrooge, speaking louder.
    'In life, I was your partner,
Jacob Marley.'   *15*
    'Will you — can you sit
down?' said Scrooge, who was
not sure about ghosts' habits.
    'I can.'
    'Do it then.'   *20*
    Scrooge had to ask this
question. He did not know
whether a ghost, which he
could see through, would be
able to sit in a chair. He felt   *25*
that impossible things always
needed an explanation. But
the ghost sat down on the op-
posite side of the fire-place.
    'You don't believe in me?'   *30*
said the ghost.

'I don't,' said Scrooge.

'You can see and hear me. Why are you afraid of your own thoughts?'

'Because a little thing can easily change their be-
5   haviour and make them strange. You may be some food I have eaten which does not agree with me. You may be a piece of fish or cake, or perhaps some badly cooked meat.'

It was not Scrooge's habit to make a joke. Certainly
10   he did not feel very happy then. The truth is, he talked like that to try to forget the cold fear he felt. The voice of the ghost had frightened him until he shook with fear.

'You see this button?' said Scrooge. He tried to take
15   the glassy eyes of his visitor away from himself.

'I do,' replied the ghost.

'But you are not looking at it,' said Scrooge.

'But I see it,' said the ghost.

'Well,' went on Scrooge, 'if I eat this, ghosts will fol-
20   low me for the rest of my life. I can make ghosts. I have no need to see you. So go away, I say.'

'You are making your own chain'

At this, the ghost gave a frightening cry, and shook its chain with a terrible noise. Scrooge held his chair tightly to keep himself from falling. Then, at last, he fell on his
25   knees. 'Oh terrible ghost,' he said, 'why do you trouble me?'

'Do you believe in me or do you not?'

'I do,' said Scrooge, 'I must. Why do ghosts walk on the earth? Why do they come to me?'

30   'The spirit* of every man must walk among other

*spirit, the part of a human being which remains after death.

men, and travel far and wide. If that spirit does not do
this in life, it must do so after death. It then journeys
round the world. It must look at things it cannot share —
things which other people can share on earth and which
make them happy.'   *5*

'Why are you wearing that chain?' asked Scrooge.

'I wear the chain I made for myself in life. I made it
piece by piece. I made it cheerfully, and I wore it cheerfully. Does its metal seem strange to you?'

Scrooge shook more and more.   *10*

'I can tell you this fact. The chain you are making
for yourself was as full and heavy as this seven years
ago. You have made it longer and heavier since then.'

Scrooge looked on the floor behind him. He was
afraid of finding the chain, but he could see nothing.   *15*

'Jacob,' he asked, 'tell me more. Give me some
comfort.'

'I have no comfort to give,' the ghost replied. 'Nor
can I tell you what I would like to. I am only allowed
a little more time. I cannot stay; I cannot rest anywhere.   *20*
In my life, my spirit never left the narrow money-
making office. Now, long journeys are before me.'

'Have you travelled very slowly then?' asked Scrooge
in a quiet business-like way.

'Slowly!'   *25*

'Seven years dead, and travelling all the time?'

'Yes, the whole time. No rest, no peace.'

It held up its chain, then threw it to the ground again.
Perhaps that chain was the cause of all its trouble. 'At
this time of the year I have most pain. Why did I walk   *30*
through crowds of other people with my eyes turned
down? Why didn't I send them to God's star, which led
the wise men to a poor home? Did its light lead me to
any poor homes?'

Scrooge was not at all happy to hear the spirit talking like this.

'Hear me,' cried the ghost, 'my time is nearly gone.'

'I will,' said Scrooge, 'but don't be too hard on me,
5 Jacob.'

'I can't tell you how I can appear before you in this shape. I have sat by you often, but you have not noticed me.'

It was not a pleasant thought. Scrooge put his hand
10 across his fore-head*.

Scrooge is given a chance

'That is part of my punishment. I am here tonight to tell you that you do not need to have pain like me. I have given you that chance, Ebenezer.'

'You were always a good friend to me,' said Scrooge,
15 'thank you, Jacob.'

'Three ghosts will visit you.' Scrooge's face showed that he was afraid of the idea.

'Is that the chance you are talking about, Jacob?' he asked in a weak voice.

20   'It is.'

'I think I would rather not,' said Scrooge.

'If they don't visit you, you will certainly become like me. Expect the first spirit tomorrow when the clock strikes one.'

25   'Couldn't I see them all at once,' suggested Scrooge, 'and finish it quickly?'

'Expect the second spirit on the second night at the same time. The third spirit on the next night at exactly twelve o'clock. You will see me no more. For your own
30 good, remember what I have told you.'

When it had said these words, the ghost stood up and walked to the window. At every step, the window rose
fore-head, front part of head.

a little. By the time the ghost reached it, the window
was wide open.

Scrooge followed and looked out. The air was full of
ghosts, each wearing a chain. As Marley's ghost joined
them, they all went out of sight in the dark, cold air.   *5*

2   The Ghost of Christmas Past

When Scrooge awoke, it was very dark. He looked out
of bed and could hardly see the window. As he tried to
see through the darkness, the bell of a nearby church
struck twelve. He was surprised, for it had been two
5   o'clock when he went to bed. He thought that the clock
was wrong.

'It can't be true!' he said, 'Have I slept through a
whole day, and far into another night? It is not possible
that anything has happened to the sun, and this is the
10   afternoon.'

Then he suddenly remembered that the ghost had
told him of a visitor when the bell had struck one. He
wanted to be awake until the hour had passed. This was
a wise thought, as he certainly could not sleep. At one

o'clock the bell sounded a deep, slow, *one.* A bright
light appeared in the room. In a second, Scrooge found
himself face to face with a visitor from another world.

It was a strange being, like a child but also like an old
man. Its hair was white like an old man's hair, but the   *5*
face was young. Its skin was fair and beautiful. The
arms and hands were long and very strong. Its legs, like
its arms, had nothing on them. It wore a dress of white,
and round it a beautiful shining belt. Although it held
a branch of fresh holly in its hand, its dress was covered   *10*
with summer flowers. The strangest thing of all was the
bright clear light coming from its head. It held, under
its arm, a long, pointed cap which, when placed on the
head, would hide the light.

'Are you the ghost I was told to expect?' said   *15*
Scrooge.

'I am.'

The voice was soft and gentle, but came from a dis-
tance instead of close beside him.

'Who and what are you?' Scrooge asked.

'I am the ghost of Christmas Past.'

'Long past?' asked Scrooge.

'No, your past.'

5   For no reason Scrooge suddenly had a strong wish. He wanted to see the spirit in his cap, and he asked him to put it on.

'What!' cried the ghost. 'Do you want me immediately to put out the fire I give? Is it not enough that you are 10 the one who made this cap? Is it not enough that, because of you, I must wear it fixed on my head?'

Scrooge said that he did not mean to hurt anyone. He did not know that he had put a cap on to any ghost. He was then brave enough to ask why the ghost had come.

15   'Because you need my help,' said the ghost. Scrooge thanked him very much, but thought that a good night's sleep was all the help he wanted. The ghost heard his thoughts, for it said at once, 'Take care!' and with its strong hand held him gently by the arm.

Scrooge makes a journey

20   'Rise and walk with me.' The hand, though gentle as a woman's, would not leave him. Scrooge rose. He found that the spirit was going to the window. He held its dress to stop it.

'I shall fall,' he said.

25   The spirit put its hand on Scrooge's heart, saying, 'I shall hold you up.'

As the words were spoken, they passed through the wall and stood upon an open road, with fields on either side.

30   They could not see the city. It was a cold, clear, winter day with snow upon the ground.

'I can't believe it!' said Scrooge as he looked around him. 'I used to live in this place. I was a boy here.'

The ghost watched him. The old man thought its gentle touch was still present.

'Your lip is shaking,' said the ghost, 'and what is that upon your face? Are you crying?'

Scrooge answered roughly that it was nothing at all. He asked the ghost to lead him where he wished. 'You remember the way,' said the ghost.

'Remember it!' cried Scrooge. 'I can find my way with my eyes shut.'

'It is strange that you had forgotten it for so many years,' said the ghost. 'Let us go on.'

They walked along the road. Scrooge knew every garden and post and tree. Then they came to a little town with a bridge and a church, and a winding river. Some boys, riding horses, came towards them. They were calling to other boys. They were all enjoying themselves and the fields were full of lovely music. Even the air laughed to hear them.

The boys came on and, as they reached him, Scrooge knew and named every one of them. Why was he so glad to see them? Why did his cold eyes shine, and his heart beat quickly as they went past? Why was he filled with joy when they wished each other a happy Christmas, and left to go to their different homes? What was a happy Christmas to Scrooge? Had he ever enjoyed Christmas?

Scrooge sees himself as a child

'The school is not quite empty,' said the spirit. 'A boy, all alone and forgotten by his friends, is still there.'

Scrooge said he knew it, and his tears fell.

They left the high road, and walked along a path Scrooge knew well. Soon they reached a house made of dark red brick. It was a large house, but it had not been cared for. The walls were wet, the windows broken and the doors wide open. Everywhere was covered with grass. The rooms were big and cold, and had poor furniture.

The ghost and Scrooge went across the hall to a door
5 at the back of the house. It opened before them, and showed a long, ugly room, with lines of wooden desks. Scrooge sat down and tried to see himself as he used to be.

Scrooge remembered every sound in the room, and
10 every movement from the tree outside. These all softened the heart of Scrooge, and made his tears fall more and more freely.

The ghost touched him on the arm, and pointed to Scrooge as a young boy, reading quietly.

15 'I wish,' Scrooge began, putting his hand into his pocket and looking about him, ' . . . but it is too late now!'

'What is the matter?' asked the ghost.

'Nothing,' said Scrooge, 'nothing. There was a boy
20 singing a Christmas carol at my door last night. I am sorry that I did not give him something; that is all.'

The ghost smiled kindly and said, 'Let's see another Christmas.'

Scrooge's old self grew larger at the words. The room
25 became a little darker and dirtier. Scrooge did not know how this happened. He only knew that it was quite right, and that everything had happened just like that. There he was, alone again, when all the other boys had gone home for their holidays. He was not reading now, but
30 walking up and down sadly. The door opened and a little girl ran in and put her arms round his neck, saying, 'Dear brother, I have come to bring you home.'

'Home, little sister?'

'Yes,' said the child, 'home for ever. Father is much
35 kinder now, and home is happy. He sent me to bring

you. You will never come back here.' She began to pull
him to the door with all her strength.
'She was never very strong,' said the ghost, 'but she
had a kind heart.'
'You are right.'   *5*
'She is dead. But she had children, didn't she?'
'One child,' Scrooge said.
'True,' said the ghost. 'Your nephew.'
Scrooge seemed worried and answered, 'Yes.'

Scrooge at Fezziwig's
They were now in the busy streets of the city, al-   *10*
though they had only just left the school. The ghost
stopped at one of the business houses, and asked Scrooge
if he knew it.
'Know it?' said Scrooge. 'I learned my business there.'
They went in. At the sight of an old gentleman sitting   *15*
behind a high desk, Scrooge cried, 'Why, it's old Fezziwig, alive again.'
Old Fezziwig put down his pen and looked at the
clock. It was seven o'clock. He rubbed his hands together
and laughed. In a comfortable, fat, happy voice, he   *20*
called out, 'Hello there, Ebenezer, Dick!'
Scrooge's old self, now a young man, came in quickly.
He was followed by another pupil, his best friend. 'Dick
Wilkins,' said Scrooge. 'Yes, there he is. He liked me
very much, did Dick. Poor Dick! So bad!'   *25*
'Hello, my boys,' cried Fezziwig, 'no more work to-
night. It is Christmas Eve, Dick! Christmas, Ebenezer!
Let's close the windows.'
You would not believe how quickly those two young
men worked. They closed and fastened the windows   *30*
quickly, and came back, breathing like race-horses.
'Hello,' cried old Fezziwig, jumping down from the

high desk. 'Clear everything away, my pupils, and let's have lots of room here. Come along Dick, and Ebenezer.'

They cleared away everything while old Fezziwig watched them. It was all done in a minute. Every table and desk was moved away, as if the room would never be an office again. The floor was brushed and cleaned, the lamps were prepared and much coal was put on the fire. The room was as comfortable and warm and bright as you would wish to see on a December night.

The musician* came in with a music-book. He was followed by Mrs Fezziwig, with a great wide smile, and the three Misses Fezziwig, laughing and beautiful. Then came the six young men who were in love with them, and then all the young men and women working in the business. In came the servant with her cousin, the baker*; in came the cook with her brother's special friend, the milkman*. In came the boy from across the road, trying to hide himself behind the girl from the next house. They all came in one after another, and started to dance. Twenty pairs at once, down the middle and up again, round and round, some always found in the wrong place. When the dance was finished, old Fezziwig clapped his hands and cried out, 'Well done!' The musician hid his face in a large drink.

There were more and more dances. There was cake and there was wine*, and there were great pieces of cold meat. After supper, the musician played the great dance of the evening. Then old Fezziwig stood up to dance with Mrs Fezziwig.

When the clock struck eleven, the party finished. Mr and Mrs Fezziwig stood on each side of the door. They

*musician, one who plays music.
*baker, a man who makes bread.
*milkman, a man who sells milk.
*wine, a strong drink.

shook hands with everyone and wished him or her a happy Christmas.

Soon everyone had gone and the cheerful voices were no longer heard. The two pupils were left alone to go to their beds at the back of the shop.

Scrooge puts out the light of Christmas Past

During this time, Scrooge had acted very strangely. His heart belonged to the party and his old self. He remembered everything, enjoyed everything, and was strangely excited. It was not until the end that he remembered the ghost. He saw that it was looking at him, while the light on its head burned very clearly.

'It's not difficult to make these simple people happy,' said the ghost.

'Simple!' said Scrooge.

He listened to the two pupils who were praising Fezziwig warmly.

'He has spent only a few pounds, three or four perhaps. Is that so very much?'

'It isn't that,' said Scrooge, speaking like his old, and not like his present, self. 'It isn't that, Ghost. He is able to make us happy or sad, to make our work heavy or light. He is strong in words and looks, in things so small that it is not possible to add them up. What then? The happiness he gives us is more than anything which a large sum of money can buy.'

He felt the ghost's eyes upon him.

'What's the matter?' asked the ghost.

'Nothing at all!' said Scrooge.

'Something, I think.'

'No,' said Scrooge, 'but I would like to say a few words to Bob Cratchit now. That's all.'

His old self turned the lamps low as he spoke this

wish. Scrooge and the ghost stood again in the open air.
'These are the *shadows* of the things that have happened.'

'Take me away,' cried Scrooge, 'show me no more.'

The ghost's light was burning high and bright. Scrooge
took hold of the pointed cap and quickly covered the   5
ghost's head. The ghost dropped beneath it, but the light
still flowed from under the cap. Scrooge pressed the cap
down until he suddenly felt very tired. He fell back and
found himself in his own bedroom again. He hardly had
time to reach the bed before he fell into a heavy sleep.   10

3   The Ghost of Christmas Present

When Scrooge woke up, he knew what time it was. No
one had to tell him that the clock was about to strike
one. He felt that he had woken up just in time. He was
ready for anything, but he did not expect nothing. So
5   when the clock struck one, and no shape appeared, he
began to shake with fear. Five minutes, ten minutes, a
quarter of an hour passed and nothing came.

But all this time, after the clock had struck the hour,
a light was shining over his bed. This light frightened
10   him more than an army of ghosts. He wanted to know
where it came from. He got up quietly, and went, in his
slippers, to the door of the next room.

As soon as his hand touched the handle, a strange
voice called him by his name and told him to enter. He
15   obeyed.

It was his own room, but it had changed surprisingly.
The walls and ceiling were covered with green leaves. It
looked like a small wood, full of shining berries*. A
great fire was burning — something that room had never
20   known in Scrooge's time nor Marley's. On the floor were
heaps of Christmas food and fruit, and bowls of warm
drink. A great happy giant* was sitting easily on top of
it all, — it was a wonderful sight. He carried a bright
light, and held it up high as Scrooge came round the
25   door.

'Come in,' cried the ghost, 'come in, and know me
better, man.'

Scrooge entered in fear and hung down his head

*berries, small coloured fruit.
*giant, a very large man.

before this ghost. He was not the same old Scrooge. The ghost's eyes were clear and kind, but he did not like to look at them.

'I am the ghost of Christmas Present,' it said. 'Look at me.' 5

Scrooge did as he was asked. It was wearing a long green dress, with white fur round it. Its feet and chest were not covered. On its head it wore some green leaves, and bright berries and shining ice. Its dark brown hair was long and free — as free as its kind face and bright 10 eyes, its open hand and its happy voice.

'Have you seen anyone like me before?' asked the spirit.

'Never,' answered Scrooge.

'Have you never walked with other members of my 15 family?'

'I don't think I have,' said Scrooge. 'I am afraid I have not. Have you had many brothers, Ghost?'

'More than eighteen hundred,' replied the spirit.

'A big family!' said Scrooge. 'Ghost, take me where 20 you want. I went out last night because another ghost took me. I learned a lesson which is working now. To-night, if you have anything to teach me, let me learn from it.'

'Touch my dress.' Scrooge did as he was told, and 25 held it tightly.

Christmas Present

The room, the fire and the dark disappeared immediately. They were standing in the city streets on a Christmas morning. The weather was very cold, and the people made a rough but pleasant noise by kicking the snow. 30 They kicked it from the paths in front of their homes, and threw it from the tops of their houses. It was great fun to the boys to see it falling down into the road below, and break up into small snow-storms.

The town itself was not very bright, but there was
happiness everywhere. The people who were clearing
away the snow were full of fun. They called out to
each other as they brushed. Sometimes they threw
5   a snow-ball at each other, laughing if it went wrong,
and laughing even louder if it went right.

The fruit-shops made a bright show. There
were baskets of shining fruit, ripe for carrying
home in paper bags and for eating after dinner.
10   And the grocers*. They were half closed,
but one could still see most pleasant sights. The
scales* were making a happy sound; the string
was cleverly tying up the parcels; the smell of tea
came pleasantly to the nose; and the cakes were
15   very rich and sweet. The coldest person watching
felt sick because he thought he had already eaten
too much!

The people in the shops were all hurrying and
very busy. They fell against each other at the
20   door, banging their baskets together. Some left
their parcels in the shops and came running
back to get them. Then they made a hundred
other little mistakes, all in the happiest way.

Christmas at Bob Cratchit's

The ghost continued, and took Scrooge
25   with him, still holding on to his dress, and
feeling kind towards all poor men. He
took him straight to Bob Cratchit's. At
the door the spirit stood for a minute
and smiled. Then he held up his hands
30   and said a prayer over the small
house. What a thought! Bob only

*grocer, one who sells tea, sugar, etc.
*scales, used by grocers to weigh things.

earned fifteen shillings a week, but the ghost of Christmas Present had said a prayer for his family!

Then they saw Mrs Cratchit, Bob's wife, poorly dressed but in bright colours. She laid the cloth on the
5   table, helped by Belinda, her second daughter. Young Peter Cratchit stuck a fork into the cooking pot, getting the corners of his great shirt-collar into his mouth. (It was Bob's collar, but lent to his son just for the day.)

Now two smaller Cratchits, a boy and a girl, came run-
10 ning in. They said that they had smelt their own goose* cooking at the baker's and thought of the good dinner to come! These two young Cratchits danced around the table. Master Peter blew on the fire until the slow pot boiled.

15   'Where is your father now?' called Mrs Cratchit. 'And your brother, Tiny Tim? And Martha was not as late as this last Christmas.'

'Here's Martha, Mother,' said Martha, appearing as she spoke.

20   'Here's Martha, Mother,' repeated the two young Cratchits. 'Hooray, Martha! The goose is so big!'

'May God protect you! You're so late,' said Mrs Cratchit, kissing her many times and taking off her coat and hat.

25   'We had a lot of work to finish last night,' replied the girl, 'and we had to clear away this morning, Mother.'

'Well, that does not matter now. I am happy that you've come,' said Mrs Cratchit. 'Sit down before the fire and make yourself warm, and may God protect you.'

30   'No, no, here's Father coming,' cried the two Cratchits, who were everywhere at once. 'Hide, Martha, hide.'

Poor Tiny Tim

So Martha hid herself, and Bob, the father, came in.
*goose, a large bird.

He had at least three feet of scarf hanging down in front of him. His thin clothes were mended and brushed because it was Christmas Day. And Tiny Tim was on his shoulder. Poor Tiny Tim could not walk much. He carried a little stick and his legs were held by pieces of iron. 5

'Why, where's our Martha?' cried Bob Cratchit, looking round.

'She's not coming,' said Mrs Cratchit.

'Not coming?' said Bob, suddenly looking unhappy. He had been Tim's horse all the way from church, and 10 had come home in great joy. 'Is she not coming home on Christmas Day?'

Martha did not like to see him looking sad, even though it was only a joke. She came out from behind the door, and ran into his arms. The two young Cratchits 15 carried Tiny Tim into the kitchen. In this way, Tiny Tim could hear the boiling pudding knocking against the pot.

'And did little Tim behave well?' asked Mrs Cratchit, when Bob had kissed his daughter and talked to her.

'Very well,' replied Bob. 'You know he has many 20 thoughts sitting by himself so much. He thinks the strangest things you have ever heard. He told me something when we were coming home. He hoped the people saw him in church, because he was lame. He wanted them to enjoy remembering who made lame men walk 25 and blind men see.'

Bob's voice was not calm when he told them this. Nor was it calm when he said that Tiny Tim was growing stronger. His happy little stick was heard upon the floor. Before another word was spoken, Tiny Tim came back, 30 with his brother and sister, to his chair by the fire. Then Bob, taking off his hat, mixed a hot drink in a jug, and put it near the fire. Young Peter and the two younger Cratchits went to fetch the goose. They soon returned with it. 35

Then they set chairs for everybody, not forgetting themselves. Bob put Tiny Tim beside him at a corner of the table. At last the dishes were put out, and the family thanked God for His kindness.

5   Then followed an exciting time, as Mrs Cratchit, looking slowly along the knife, started to cut the goose. When she did this, a sound of joy arose all round. Even Tiny Tim, excited by the two young Cratchits, beat the table with

10   his knife and cried 'Hurrah!'

There was never such a large goose. Bob said he did not believe there ever would be another like this. It was enough to feed the whole family. Mrs Cratchit looked at the

15   small piece left on the dish. Indeed, she said with happiness that they had not eaten it all! Yet everyone had had enough, and the plates were changed by Miss Belinda.

20   Mrs Cratchit then left the room alone, because she did not wish the family to watch her. She put the pudding on the dish and brought it in. Was it cooked enough?

25   Would it break when taken from the dish on to the table? Had someone climbed over the wall and stolen it while they were eating the goose?

30   The two young Cratchits went pale at the thought. They thought of all sorts of troubles.

What a lot of steam!

35   The pudding was out

of the pot. A smell like washing-day! That was the cloth around the pudding. A smell like a restaurant with a baker's next door and a wash-house next door to that. That was the pudding. In half a minute Mrs Cratchit
5 entered. She was rather red but smiled proudly. The pudding was like a ball with spots, brown and hard. The lighted brandy flamed round it, and a piece of holly was stuck in the top.

'Oh, a wonderful pudding!' Bob said, and he meant it
10 too. It was the greatest success Mrs Cratchit had had since their marriage. Everybody had something to say about it. Nobody, though, said that they thought it was a small pudding for a large family. No Cratchit would even think this sort of thing!

15 At last the dinner was all finished. The cloth was cleared and the fire made up. The drink which Bob had mixed was tasted; it was just right.

Apples and pears were put on the table. All the family sat round the fire in what Bob called a circle, but he
20 meant half a circle. At his side were the family glasses — two large glasses and a cup without a handle. These held the hot drink better than cups of gold. Bob poured it for them with a smiling face, and then said, 'A Happy Christmas to us all, my dears, God look upon us!' And
25 the family said the same.

Will Tiny Tim live?

'God look upon us all,' said Tiny Tim the last of the family. He sat very close to his father's side upon his little chair. Bob held his hand in his because he loved the child, and wished to keep him by his side, and feared
30 that God might take him from this world.

'Ghost,' said Scrooge, with an interest he had never felt before, 'tell me if Tiny Tim will live.'

'I see an empty chair,' replied the ghost, 'in the

corner, and a small stick without its owner. If this does
not change in the future, the child will die.'

'No, no,' said Scrooge, 'oh no, kind ghost, say that he
will live.'

'If next Christmas we do not find him here, what
then? If he is likely to die, he must do it, and make the
numbers of poor people smaller.'

Scrooge hung his head to hear his own words said
again by the ghost. But he lifted it quickly as he heard
his own name.

'Mr Scrooge!' said Bob. 'We will drink in the name of
Mr Scrooge who gave us the dinner.'

'Gave us the dinner?' said Mrs Cratchit, going very
red. 'I wish he were here. I would tell him a few things
to feed upon, and I hope he would enjoy it.'

'My dear,' said Bob, 'it is Christmas Day!'

'I will drink to his health because of you and today,
but not because of him. Long life to him, a Happy
Christmas and a Happy New Year. He'll certainly be
very joyful, and very happy!'

The children drank after her. It was the first thing
they had done without joy. Tiny Tim drank the last of
all. The name of Scrooge had thrown a dark shadow on
to the party, which did not leave for five minutes. Afterwards they were ten times happier than before. Now
they had finished with Scrooge.

They were not a good-looking family. They were not
well-dressed; their shoes did not keep out the wet weather; their clothes were poor and thin. But they were
happy and kind and pleased with one another. Scrooge
watched them all, but especially Tiny Tim, to the last.

Christmas at Scrooge's nephew's house

By this time it was getting dark, and snowing rather
heavily. As Scrooge and the ghost went along the streets,

the bright flames of the fires in the houses were wonderful. Children were running out to be the first to greet their married sisters, brothers, uncles, aunts. Many people were on their way to friendly parties. Perhaps there
5　was no one at home to greet them!

What a kind ghost! He led Scrooge to where men worked deep down in the earth, and to those in country fields. Even over the sea, to where sailors sang their Christmas songs, and each remembered those he loved
10　far away.

While Scrooge was thinking about these sights, he heard a loud happy laugh. It was a great surprise to him, and it was an even greater surprise to know that it was his nephew's laugh. Then he found himself in a bright
15　room. The spirit was smiling by his side, and looking with joy at the nephew.

'Ha, ha, ha,' laughed Scrooge's nephew. 'Ha, ha, ha!'

Perhaps you may know a man with a happier laugh than Scrooge's nephew. All I can say is that I should like
20　to know him too! Bring him to me and I'll make him my friend. Illness and bad fortune spread, but nothing spreads so easily and so quickly as laughter and joy. Scrooge's nephew laughed in this way, holding his sides and rolling his head. Scrooge's niece laughed as much as
25　he did. And his friends laughed out too.

They talk about Scrooge

'He said that Christmas was nonsense, and he believed it too!' cried Scrooge's nephew.

'More bad fortune on him, Fred,' said Scrooge's niece.

She was very pretty, with a gentle, surprised-looking
30　face, a sweet little mouth, and the sunniest pair of eyes you ever saw in any person's head.

'He's a strange old man,' said Scrooge's nephew,

'that's the truth, and not really very pleasant either. However, his habits carry their own punishment, and I have nothing to say against him.'

'I'm sure he's very rich, Fred,' said Scrooge's niece, 'at least that is what you always tell me.' 5

'What is that, my dear?' said Scrooge's nephew. 'His money is of no use to him. He does not do any good with it. He does not even make himself comfortable with it. He has not the joy of thinking, ha, ha, that it is ever going to help me.' 10

'I have no time for him,' said Scrooge's niece. Scrooge's niece's sisters and all the other ladies thought the same.

'Oh, I have,' said Scrooge's nephew. 'I am sorry for him. If I really tried I would be angry with him. He only makes himself sad by his bad behaviour. He decides not 15 to like us, so he won't come to dinner with us. What happens? He does not lose much of a dinner!'

'No, I think he loses a very good dinner,' said Scrooge's niece. Everybody else said the same, and they were right. They had just finished dinner, and, with the wine and 20 sweets and fruit upon the table, they were sitting round the fire in the lamplight.

'Well, I'm glad to hear it,' said Scrooge's nephew, 'for I do not like young servants! What do you say, Topper?'

Topper had clearly fallen in love with one of Scrooge's 25 niece's sisters. He answered that as a bachelor* he was unable to give his ideas on the question. At this, Scrooge's niece's sister, the fat one in the silk dress, not the pretty one, went very red.

'Do go on, Fred,' said Scrooge's niece, 'he never 30 finishes what he begins to say.'

Scrooge's nephew enjoyed another loud laugh. His example was followed by everyone.

*bachelor, a man who is not married.

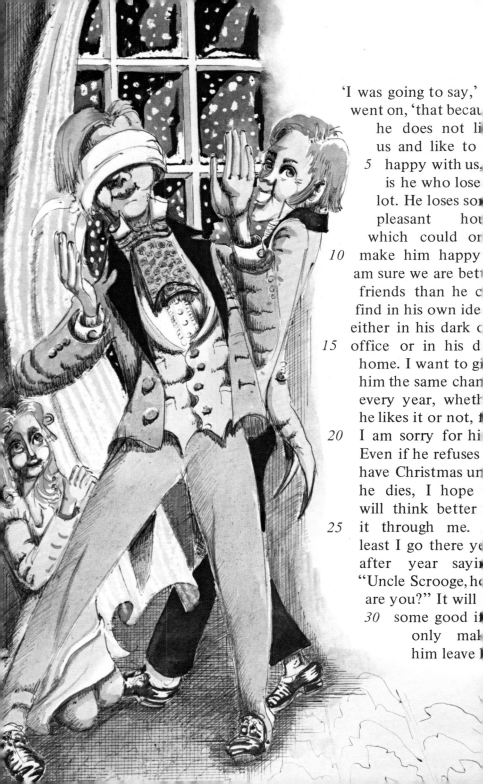

'I was going to say,'
went on, 'that becau
    he does not li
    us and like to
5 happy with us,
    is he who lose
    lot. He loses so
    pleasant   hou
    which could or
10 make him happy
    am sure we are bet
    friends than he c
    find in his own ide
    either in his dark
15 office or in his d
    home. I want to gi
    him the same chan
    every year, wheth
    he likes it or not, f
20 I am sorry for hi
    Even if he refuses
    have Christmas un
    he dies, I hope
    will think better
25 it through me.
    least I go there ye
    after year sayi
    "Uncle Scrooge, h
    are you?" It will
30 some good i
    only mak
    him leave l

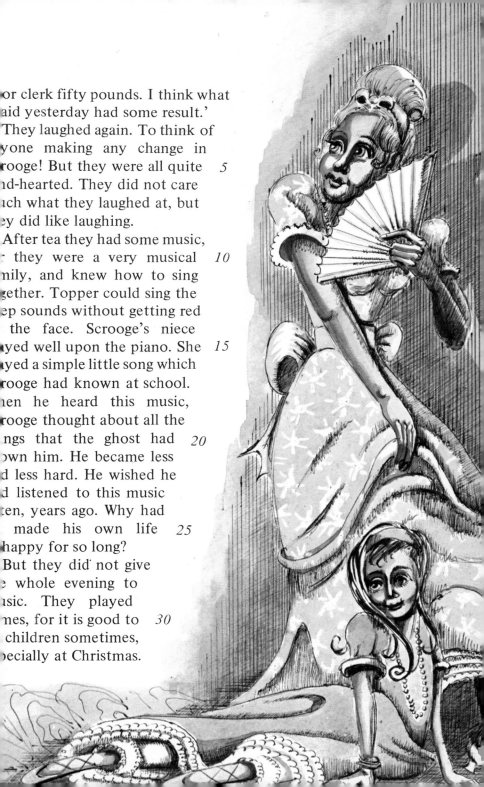

or clerk fifty pounds. I think what
aid yesterday had some result.'
They laughed again. To think of
yone making any change in
rooge! But they were all quite   5
id-hearted. They did not care
ich what they laughed at, but
ey did like laughing.

After tea they had some music,
 they were a very musical   10
nily, and knew how to sing
gether. Topper could sing the
ep sounds without getting red
 the face. Scrooge's niece
iyed well upon the piano. She   15
iyed a simple little song which
rooge had known at school.
ien he heard this music,
rooge thought about all the
ngs that the ghost had   20
own him. He became less
d less hard. He wished he
d listened to this music
ten, years ago. Why had
 made his own life   25
happy for so long?
But they did' not give
 whole evening to
isic. They played
nes, for it is good to   30
children sometimes,
iecially at Christmas.

Christmas games

There was a game of *Blind-man's buff**. And I cannot believe that Topper really could not see. You should have seen the way he went after that fat sister in the silk dress! He knocked over the table, fell over the chairs
5   and hit the piano. Wherever she went, he went too. He always knew where that sister was! He would not catch anyone else. Some of them fell against him, but he did not catch them! He went away at once following that fat sister. She often cried out that it was not fair, and it
10 really was not. And when at last he caught her, he pretended he did not know who she was!

The ghost was very pleased to find Scrooge so interested. He was happy to hear him ask like a child, to stay until the end of the party. But the ghost said he
15 could not do this.

'Here is a new game,' said Scrooge, 'one half-hour more, ghost, please!'

It was a game called *Yes and no*. Scrooge's nephew had to think of something, and the rest must find out
20 what it was. He could only answer *Yes* or *No* to their questions.

He was asked many questions. They found that he was thinking of an animal. A live animal; an animal which was not pleasant; a fighting animal; an animal that talked
25 sometimes; lived in London and walked along the streets; not shown to the public; not led by anybody; did not live in a zoo; was never killed in a market; was not a horse, a donkey, a cow, a tiger, a dog, a pig, or a cat.

Every time a question was put to him, this nephew
30 laughed again. He was so amused that he had to stand up. At last the fat sister in the silk dress called out, 'I have found it, Fred, I know what it is.'

**Blind-man's buff*, a game where one player, with his eyes covered, tries to catch another player.

'What is it?' asked Fred.

'It's your Uncle Scroo—o—o—oge.'

And it certainly was. Everybody thought Scrooge's nephew was very clever. Some now said that the answer to 'Is it a tiger?' was 'Yes'. 5

'He has given us plenty of fun, I'm sure,' said Fred, 'and so it is unkind if we do not drink to his health. Here is a glass of wine, I drink to the health of Uncle Scrooge.'

'To Uncle Scrooge,' they cried. 10

'A Happy Christmas, and a Happy New Year to the old man, whatever he is,' said Scrooge's nephew. 'He would not take it from me, but yet he may have it. Uncle Scrooge.'

Uncle Scrooge had become happy and light-hearted. 15 He wanted to thank them in a speech, but the ghost did not give him time. The whole room passed away with the last word. He and the spirit were again upon their travels.

The ghost grows older

They saw much and they went far. They visited many 20 homes, but always with a happy result. The ghost stood beside sick people and they became cheerful. He stood in foreign lands, and they seemed close at home. He stood by poor men and they felt rich. He went to work-houses, and hospitals, and prisons, and left his happiness 25 there.

It was a long night. But Scrooge was not sure if it was only one night. He thought one thing was very strange. He himself did not change in his face and body, but the ghost grew clearly older. 30

'Are ghosts' lives so short?' asked Scrooge. He looked at the ghost as they stood together in an open space, and he noticed that its hair was grey.

'My life upon this earth is very short,' replied the ghost, 'it ends tonight.'

'Tonight!' cried Scrooge.

'Tonight, at midnight; the time is coming close.'

5 They heard the church bell striking a quarter to midnight. Very soon after, the bell struck twelve.

Scrooge looked about him for the ghost, and did not see it. On the last sound of the bell, he remembered the third visitor of which Jacob Marley had spoken. He 10 lifted up his eyes, and saw something covered from head to foot in black. Another ghost was coming, like a cloud, along the ground towards him.

4   The Ghost of Christmas in the Future

By this time, Scrooge was used to ghosts as companions.
But he feared the silent shape very much. His legs shook
beneath him. He could hardly stand when he prepared
to follow it. The ghost waited a minute to give him extra
time.   5

But Scrooge felt even worse. He was filled with an un-
certain fear because he knew that, behind the black
clothes, there were eyes which could see him. Although
he tried very hard, he himself could see nothing but an
out-stretched hand, and a black shape.   10

'Are you the Ghost of Christmas in the Future?' he
asked. 'I fear you more than any spirit I have seen. But
I know that your purpose is to do me good, and I hope
to become a better man than I was. I am prepared to
come with you, and to do so with a thankful heart. Will   15
you not speak to me?'

The ghost gave him no reply. The hand was pointed
straight before him.

'Continue,' said Scrooge, 'continue. The night is going
quickly, and time is short for me. Lead on, Spirit.'   20

The ghost moved past Scrooge in the way in which it
had come. Scrooge followed in the shadow of its dress,
which lifted him up and carried him along.

They did not enter the city, but the city grew up
around them. But there they were, standing in the centre   25
of it. Businessmen hurried up and down the street, and
looked carefully at their watches, as Scrooge had seen
them do often.

Who has died?

'No,' said a great fat man, 'I don't know much about it. I only know he's dead.'

'When did he die?'

'Last night, I believe.'

'Why, what was the matter with him?' asked a third   *5*
man. 'I thought he would never die.'

'Who knows?' said the first.

'What has he done with his money?' asked a man with a very red face.

'I have not heard,' said the other man. 'Left it to his   *10*
business, perhaps. He hasn't left it to me. That's all I know.'

This joke was received with a loud laugh.

'They are going to bury him very cheaply,' said the same man. 'For I don't know anyone who will go to his   *15*
funeral. Perhaps we should make up a party and go.'

'I don't mind if there is food, but I must eat well if I go.'

Another laugh.

People who spoke and listened walked away and   *20*
mixed with others. Scrooge knew the men, and looked to the spirit for an explanation.

The ghost went on into a street. Its finger pointed to two people. Scrooge listened again, thinking the explanation might lie here. He knew these men also. They   *25*
were businessmen, very rich, and of great importance. He wanted them to think well of him, but only from a business point of view.

'How are you?' said one.

'How are you?' replied the other.   *30*

'Well, the old miser* has died at last.'

'I have heard,' answered the other. 'Cold, isn't it?'

*miser, one who saves money and lives poorly.

'It usually is at Christmas. Are you going away?'
'No, I have something else to think of. Good morning.'

The Death of Tiny Tim

The ghost led him through several streets, and Scrooge
looked here and there to find himself, but he was no-
5   where to be seen.

They entered Bob Cratchit's house which they had
visited before, and found the mother and the children
sitting round the fire.

It was quiet. Very quiet. The noisy little Cratchits
10   were quite still in one corner, and sat looking up at
Peter, who had a book before him. The mother and her
daughters were sewing. But certainly, they were all very
quiet.

'And he set a little child among them.'
Where had Scrooge heard those words? He had not
15   dreamed them? Did the boy read them out as he and the
ghost entered the house? Why did he not go on?

The mother laid her work on the table and put her
hands to her face. 'The colour hurts my eyes,' she said.
'It makes them weak by lamplight. I wouldn't like to
20   show weak eyes to your father when he comes home.
It is near his time now.'

'Past it, rather,' said Peter, shutting up his book, 'but
I think he has walked a little slower than usual these last
few evenings, Mother.'

25   They were very quiet again. At last she said, and in a
cheerful voice, 'I have known him walk, with Tiny Tim
upon his shoulder, very fast indeed.'

'I have also, often,' cried Peter.

'And we too,' cried all.

30   'But he was so very light to carry,' she went on, bent

over her work, 'and his father loved him. It was no
trouble, no trouble. Ah, here is your father at the door.'

She hurried out to meet him, and little Bob with his
scarf, which he needed, came in. His tea was ready for
him by the fire, and they all tried to help him with it.   5
Then the two young Cratchits climbed on to his knees
and laid their faces against his. They did not speak, but
they wanted to say, 'Don't be sad, Father.'

Bob was very cheerful with them and spoke very
pleasantly to all the family. He looked at the work on   10
the table, and praised what they had done. They would
be finished before Sunday, he said.

'Sunday! You went today, Robert?' asked his wife.

'Yes, my dear,' answered Bob, 'I wish you had come
there. You will be so happy to see how green the place   15
is. But then you'll see it often. I promised him I would
walk there on a Sunday. My little, little child,' cried
Bob, 'my little child.' He began to cry suddenly. He
couldn't help it.

They sat by the fire and talked, the girls and the   20
mother still sewing. Bob told them of the kindness of
Mr Scrooge's nephew. He had only seen him once. When
the nephew met him in the street that day, and seeing
that he looked a little sad, he asked what was the matter.

'Then indeed,' said Bob, 'I told him. "I am very sorry   25
about it, Mr Cratchit," he said, "and deeply sorry for
your good wife." I don't know how he knew that.'

'Knew what, my dear?'

'Why, that you were a good wife.'

'Everybody knows that,' said Peter.   30

'Very well said, my boy,' said Bob. 'I hope they do.
"Deeply sorry for your good wife. If I can be of help to
you in any way," he said, giving me his card, "that's
where I live. Please come to me." Now it wasn't because
of anything he might do for me, but more because of   35

his kind heart. I felt he had known our Tiny Tim and
that his thoughts were with us.'

'I'm sure he's a good man,' said Mrs Cratchit.

'You would be more sure of it, my dear,' said Bob,
5 'if you saw and spoke to him. I will not be surprised
if he gets Peter a better job.'

'Did you hear that, Peter?' said Mrs Cratchit.

'Well,' said Bob, 'when we must leave each other one
day, I am sure none of us shall forget Tiny Tim, shall
10 we, or this first goodbye that there was among us?'

'Never, Father,' they all cried.

'And I know, my dears,' said Bob, 'that we remember how patient and gentle he was, although he was a little child. We shall not quarrel easily among ourselves, and forget poor Tiny Tim in doing it.'

'No, never, Father,' they all cried again.   5

'I am very happy,' said Bob. 'I am very happy.'

Mrs Cratchit kissed him, his daughters kissed him, the two young Cratchits kissed him, and Peter and he shook hands.

Scrooge learns the name of the dead man

'Spirit,' said Scrooge, 'something tells me that the   10 hour when we must leave is near. I know it, but I don't know how. Tell me the name of the man whose death was spoken about.'

The Ghost of Christmas in the Future moved forward. It reached the street where Scrooge's business house   15 was. As they passed, Scrooge looked through the window. The man sitting in his chair was not himself.

He followed the ghost until they reached a high gate. He looked round before entering. A churchyard*! Here, then, was the man whose name he was going to learn.   20 The spirit stood among the graves* and pointed down to one. Scrooge went nearer, shaking as he went, and following the finger, read upon the stone of the rough grave his own name, EBENEZER SCROOGE.

The finger pointed from the grave to him and back   25 again.

'No, Spirit, oh no, no, no!'

'Spirit,' he cried, 'listen to me. I am not the man I was. Why do you show me this if there is no hope for me?'   30

*churchyard, a place where the dead are buried.
*grave, where each person is buried.

For the first time the hand appeared to shake.

'Good Spirit,' Scrooge went on, as he knelt on the ground, 'you are sorry for me. Tell me that I can still change what you have shown me, by a new life.'

5 The kind hand shook again.

'I shall love Christmas and look forward to it, and try to think of it all the year. I will live in the past, the present, and the future. I will not shut out the lessons that they teach. Oh tell me that I can rub out the writing
10 on this stone.'

In his pain he took hold of the hand. It tried to pull free. But he held it until the ghost began to change — and he found himself holding the bed-post of his own bed.

5   Scrooge Wakes up on Christmas Morning

Yes, it was his own bed-post, and the bed was his own and the room was his own. Best of all, the time before him was his own.

'I will live in the past, the present, and the future,' he said again, as he jumped out of bed. 'Oh, Jacob Marley, 5 I thank heaven and Christmas-time for this. I say it on my knees, old Jacob, on my knees.'

He was so full of his new ideas that he could hardly speak. In his last minutes with the ghost he was crying and his face was wet with tears. He was busy putting on 10 his clothes as he laughed through his tears. 'I am as light as a feather. I am as happy as a child. I am as cheerful as a schoolboy. A Happy Christmas to everybody. A Happy New Year to all the world.'

He danced into his other room. 'Ha, ha, ha!' he 15 laughed, and for a man out of practice for so many years it was an excellent laugh. The first of many excellent laughs. 'I don't know what day it is,' he cried, 'I don't know anything. Hello there!' Running to the window he opened it, and put out his head — a clear bright 20 healthy cold day, sweet fresh air, golden sunlight.

'What's today?' cried Scrooge, calling down to a boy who was dressed in his Sunday clothes.

'Eh?' replied the boy.

'What's today, my fine friend?' said Scrooge again. 25

'Today?' replied the boy. 'It's Christmas Day!'

'It's Christmas Day,' said Scrooge to himself, 'and I have not missed it. The spirits all came in one night. They can do anything they like, indeed they can. Hello, my fine friend.' 30

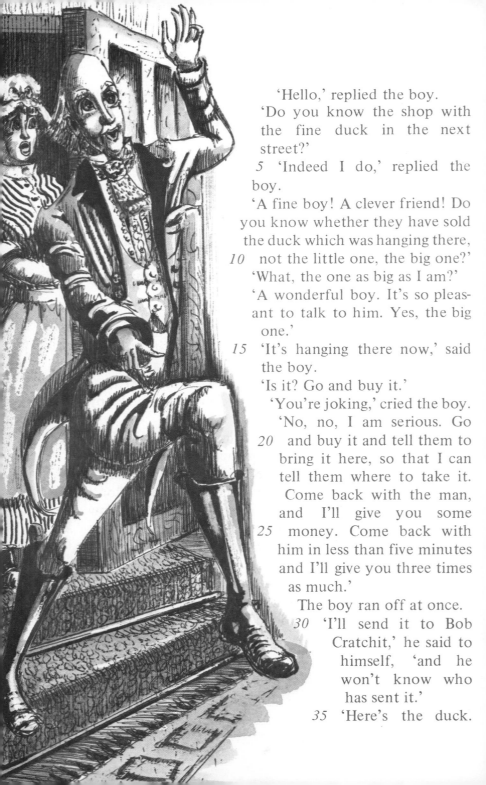

'Hello,' replied the boy.

'Do you know the shop with the fine duck in the next street?'

5 'Indeed I do,' replied the boy.

'A fine boy! A clever friend! Do you know whether they have sold the duck which was hanging there,
10 not the little one, the big one?'

'What, the one as big as I am?'

'A wonderful boy. It's so pleasant to talk to him. Yes, the big one.'

15 'It's hanging there now,' said the boy.

'Is it? Go and buy it.'

'You're joking,' cried the boy.

'No, no, I am serious. Go
20 and buy it and tell them to bring it here, so that I can tell them where to take it. Come back with the man, and I'll give you some
25 money. Come back with him in less than five minutes and I'll give you three times as much.'

The boy ran off at once.
30 'I'll send it to Bob Cratchit,' he said to himself, 'and he won't know who has sent it.'

35 'Here's the duck.

It's not possible to carry that to Camden Town, you must take a cab*.'

He laughed as he said this, and he 5 laughed as he paid for the duck. He even laughed as he paid for the cab. Everything about him gave 10 him happiness.

He dressed himself in his best clothes, and at last got into the 15 street. He had not gone far when he met the gentleman who had walked into his office the day before and said, 'Scrooge 20 and Marley, I believe.'

'My dear sir,' he said, taking the man by both his hands, 25 'how do you do? I hope you had a successful day yesterday. And will you be so 30 kind — ' here Scrooge whispered into his ear.

cab, a vehicle pulled by horses which served as a taxi in those days.

'Good heavens!' cried the gentleman, so surprised he had little breath. 'Mr Scrooge, are you serious?'

'If you please,' said Scrooge, 'all of it.'

5 'My dear sir,' said the other, shaking Scrooge by the hand, 'I do not know what to say to such kindness.'

'Don't say anything, please. I am grateful to you and I thank you fifty times.'

He went to Church, and then he watched the people going up and down in the streets. In the afternoon he 10 turned his steps to his nephew's house. He passed the door twelve times because he was afraid to knock, but at last he did it.

Scrooge visits his nephew

'Is your master at home, my dear?' he said to the girl.

'He's in the dining-room. I'll take you there.'

15 'Thank you, he knows me,' said Scrooge, with his hand on the dining-room door. 'I'll go in here.'

He opened the door quietly, and first put his head round the door. His nephew and niece were looking at the table to see that everything was right.

20 'Fred!' said Scrooge.

They were so surprised! 'Good heavens!' cried Fred. 'Who's that?'

'It's I, your Uncle Scrooge. I've come to dinner. May I come in?'

25 They were so pleased to see him that Scrooge nearly had his hand shaken off. He felt at home in five minutes. Everyone looked just the same when they came in. Wonderful party! Wonderful games! Wonderful happiness!

The next day

30 He went to the office early the next morning. He wanted to catch Bob coming late. That was what he

wanted most. And he did it. The clock struck nine, no Bob! A quarter past! No Bob! He was a full eighteen minutes late. Scrooge sat with his door wide open where he could see him come in.

Bob sat on his stool without wasting a second, and began writing very fast.

'Hello,' Scrooge called in his usual voice as near as he could make it, 'what do you mean by coming at this time of the day?'

'I am sorry,' said Bob. 'I am late.'

'You are, yes, I think you are. Come in here, please.'

'It is only once a year,' cried Bob, 'and it will not happen again. I was rather happy yesterday.'

'Now, I'll tell you something, my friend,' said Scrooge. 'I am not going to allow this sort of thing any longer, and therefore,' he said. He jumped from his chair and squeezed Bob's arm. 'And therefore, I am going to increase your pay.'

Bob nearly fell through the door. He reached for his ruler, thinking that his master was going mad.

'A Happy Christmas, Bob. A happier Christmas than I have given you for many a year. I'll increase your pay and help your family, and we will talk these matters over this afternoon. And now, Bob, make up the fires and buy some more coal before you write another letter.'

Scrooge did everything he had promised. He did it all and more. He became a good friend, a good master, and the best man that the good old city knew. Some people laughed at him, but he let them laugh. His own heart laughed, and that was good enough for him.

He had no more talks with any ghosts. People always said that he knew how to really enjoy Christmas. If only that could be said of everyone!

And so, as Tiny Tim said, 'May God care for all of us.'

Questions

Chapter 5

1. Where did Scrooge send the duck?
2. What happened when Scrooge went to his nephew's house?
3. Why was Bob Cratchit frightened when he arrived at the office?
4. How did Scrooge surprise Bob Cratchit?

Oxford Progressive English Readers

Introductory Grade

Vocabulary restricted to 1400 headwords
Illustrated in full colour

The Call of the Wild and Other Stories	Jack London
Emma	Jane Austen
Jungle Book Stories	Rudyard Kipling
Life Without Katy and Seven Other Stories	O. Henry
Little Women	Louisa M. Alcott
The Lost Umbrella of Kim Chu	Eleanor Estes
Tales from the Arabian Nights	Retold by Rosemary Border
Treasure Island	R.L. Stevenson

Grade 1

Vocabulary restricted to 2100 headwords
Illustrated in full colour

The Adventures of Sherlock Holmes	Sir Arthur Conan Doyle
Alice's Adventures in Wonderland	Lewis Carroll
A Christmas Carol	Charles Dickens
The Dagger and Wings and Other Father Brown Stories	G.K. Chesterton
The Flying Heads and Other Strange Stories	Retold by C. Nancarrow
The Golden Touch and Other Stories	Retold by R. Border
Great Expectations	Charles Dickens
Gulliver's Travels	Jonathan Swift
Hijacked!	J.M. Marks
Jane Eyre	Charlotte Brontë
Lord Jim	Joseph Conrad
Oliver Twist	Charles Dickens
The Stone Junk	Retold by D.H. Howe
Stories of Shakespeare's Plays 1	Retold by N. Kates
Tales from Tolstoy	Retold by R.D. Binfield
The Talking Tree and Other Stories	David McRobbie
The Treasure of the Sierra Madre	B. Traven
True Grit	Charles Portis

Grade 2

Vocabulary restricted to 3100 headwords
Illustrated in colour

The Adventures of Tom Sawyer	Mark Twain
Alice's Adventures through the Looking Glass	Lewis Carroll
Around the World in Eighty Days	Jules Verne
Border Kidnap	J.M. Marks
David Copperfield	Charles Dickens
Five Tales	Oscar Wilde
Fog and Other Stories	Bill Lowe
Further Adventures of Sherlock Holmes	Sir Arthur Conan Doyle

Grade 2 (cont.)

The Hound of the Baskervilles	Sir Arthur Conan Doyle
The Missing Scientist	S.F. Stevens
The Red Badge of Courage	Stephen Crane
Robinson Crusoe	Daniel Defoe
Seven Chinese Stories	T.J. Sheridan
Stories of Shakespeare's Plays 2	Retold by Wyatt & Fullerton
A Tale of Two Cities	Charles Dickens
Tales of Crime and Detection	Retold by G.F. Wear
Two Boxes of Gold and Other Stories	Charles Dickens

Grade 3

Vocabulary restricted to 3700 headwords
Illustrated in colour

Battle of Wits at Crimson Cliff	Retold by Benjamin Chia
Dr Jekyll and Mr Hyde and Other Stories	R.L. Stevenson
From Russia, with Love	Ian Fleming
The Gifts and Other Stories	O. Henry & Others
The Good Earth	Pearl S. Buck
Journey to the Centre of the Earth	Jules Verne
Kidnapped	R.L. Stevenson
King Solomon's Mines	H. Rider Haggard
Lady Precious Stream	S.I. Hsiung
The Light of Day	Eric Ambler
Moonraker	Ian Fleming
The Moonstone	Wilkie Collins
A Night of Terror and Other Strange Tales	Guy De Maupassant
Seven Stories	H.G. Wells
Stories of Shakespeare's Plays 3	Retold by H.G. Wyatt
Tales of Mystery and Imagination	Edgar Allan Poe
20,000 Leagues Under the Sea	Jules Verne
The War of the Worlds	H.G. Wells
The Woman in White	Wilkie Collins
Wuthering Heights	Emily Brontë
You Only Live Twice	Ian Fleming

Grade 4

Vocabulary within a 5000 headwords range
Illustrated in black and white

The Diamond as Big as the Ritz and Other Stories	F. Scott Fitzgerald
Dragon Seed	Pearl S. Buck
Frankenstein	Mary Shelley
The Mayor of Casterbridge	Thomas Hardy
Pride and Prejudice	Jane Austen
The Stalled Ox and Other Stories	Saki
The Thimble and Other Stories	D.H. Lawrence